# Staying Alive

Written by
John Townsend

Some parts of the world are very hot and dry.

They are too hot and dry for many plants and animals to live there.

It can be so hot you could fry an egg on a rock.

Some parts of the world are very cold and dry.

We call all these dry places deserts. Deserts can be hot or cold. Some deserts are very hot during the day and very cold at night.

It may not rain for years in a desert.

A hot, dry desert. Not many animals and plants can live here.

We all need water to live. It is too dry in deserts for most plants and animals, because there is not enough water there for them to survive.

Some animals can live with very little water. Some just don't need much water to live.
Other animals can store lots of water in their bodies. They use this water when there is nothing for them to drink. It's like carrying your own water supplies.

A kangaroo rat can live with hardly any water.
It eats dry seeds and it does not need to drink.

**Why?**
These rats have special bodies.
Their kidneys don't need fresh water. This rat can reuse its body's old water.
A clever trick!

Frogs soon die if they are away from water. They must keep their skin damp at all times.

So can a frog live in a desert?

*Yes!*

One kind of frog can store water in its body.

This 'water-holding frog' lives in a desert. It stays alive for months under the sand.

The frog fills its body with water when it rains.

Then it digs under the sand to sleep. It only wakes up when it rains again. Then it pops up for a water top-up!

This huge area of land in North Africa is called the Sahara Desert.

Thirty different types of scorpion live in this desert.

Scorpions must hunt for their food. They have two large claws to catch small animals.

Scorpions also have a long tail with a sharp tip. The tip has poison in it. They use this tail to sting insects and small animals.

Scorpions feed on insects. When they eat them, they suck the juices out of the insects. They use the water in these juices. So the scorpions can stay alive without extra water.

Some scorpions eat each other. Yum!

Scorpions also keep out of the sun. In the daytime they dig under the sand and stay there.
At night, when it is cool, they come out to hunt and to feed. It is also safer for them to hunt for food in the dark.

Most animals sweat when it is very hot. This stops the animals getting too hot. But sweating means that the animals lose some water through their skin.

Camels don't sweat very much, so they don't lose much water through their skin. This means that they can go for weeks without a drink. It helps them stay alive in deserts.

When a camel finds water, it drinks deeply. A thirsty camel can fill up with as many as 135 litres of water in about 13 minutes. This keeps it going for a long time!

A camel's hump is full of fat. If it needs to, the camel can use this fat for food and to make water. That helps it stay alive when there is nothing to eat or drink.

Staying alive in a desert can be easy for some!